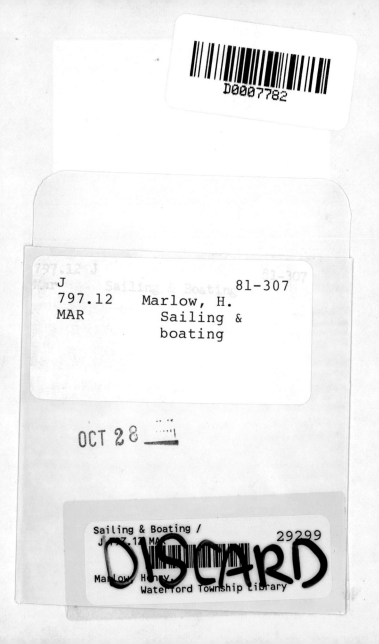

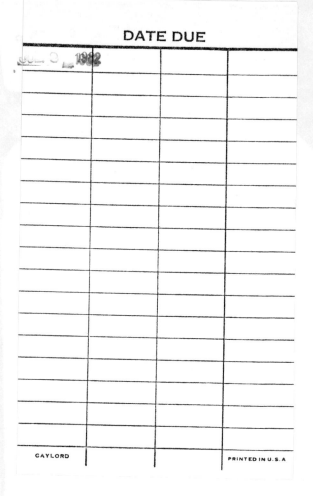

DATE DUE

JUN 0 _ 1982			

GAYLORD

PRINTED IN U.S.A

The publishers wish to acknowledge the assistance of Mr. J. E. Powell, F.R.I.N.A., when preparing this book.

Sailing and Boating

by HENRY MARLOW

with illustrations by B. H. ROBINSON

Publishers: Ladybird Books Ltd . Loughborough
© Ladybird Books Ltd (formerly Wills & Hepworth Ltd) 1972
Printed in England

Boats of all shapes and sizes

More and more people are spending their leisure hours on the water in boats of all shapes and sizes, from the fabulous seagoing yachts and cruisers through an enormous variety of smaller craft down to the modest dinghy or canoe. The size or type of boat you have does not matter so long as you enjoy what you are doing in a boat that best suits you and your pocket.

Sailing is undoubtedly the most popular form of boating as well as being one of the less expensive, and it is the purpose of this book to give you the sort of information that will start you off on this extremely enjoyable, satisfying and skilled pastime. We shall be dealing mainly with the smaller dinghies, the kind that can be carried on a car roof or easily towed behind on a light trailer. The larger, heavier and more expensive 'class' boats can wait until you are a more experienced sailor.

Dinghies are traditionally made of wood, painted or varnished, but nowadays fibreglass and plastics are being used increasingly and, of course, there are several makes of rubberised inflatables available. Most dinghies can be rowed, or powered by an outboard motor as well as sailed, and we shall briefly touch on these forms of propulsion later on.

4

0 7214 0302 6

FOLK BOAT

DRAGON

FLYING 15

MERLIN ROCKET

NATIONAL 12

MIRROR

ENTERPRISE

CADET

The dinghy

First, we must get to know the more important parts of our dinghy and the correct terms used to refer to them. The front of the boat is the *bow* and the back is the *stern*. The terms *fore* (forward) and *aft* (after) refer to the front and rear sections of the boat respectively; the centre is the *midships* portion. When facing toward the bow, the left-hand side is the *port* side and the right is the *starboard* side. The point of greatest width is the *beam*.

The main shell of the boat is called the *hull*, the top edge of which is the *gunwale* (pronounced gunnel) and the centrepiece running lengthways under the hull is the *keel*. Dinghies built primarily for sailing usually have an additional, retractable keel known as the *centreboard* or *centreplate*. This is a flat piece of wood or metal, contained within a *centreboard case*, which can be lowered through the bottom of the boat to prevent it 'slipping' sideways in the water. Seats, known as *thwarts*, are usually fitted across a dinghy so that it can be rowed when required.

A sailing boat is steered by means of a *rudder*. This is fitted on *pintles* (hinges) at the flat part of the stern, i.e., the *transom*, and can be turned by the *helmsman* in the required direction using the *tiller* (handle).

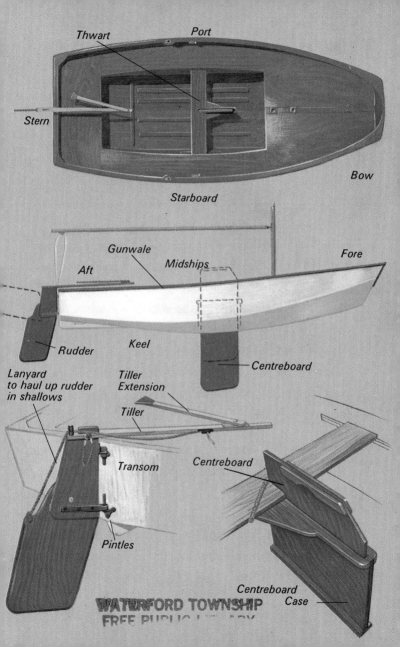

Thwart

Port

Stern

Bow

Starboard

Gunwale

Midships

Fore

Aft

Rudder

Keel

Centreboard

Lanyard
to haul up rudder
in shallows

Tiller
Extension

Tiller

Centreboard

Transom

Pintles

Centreboard
Case

The sails

Dinghies may be designed for operation with one or two sails and there are several types of sail in general use. However, as we are just beginners in the art of sailing we will start in a single-sail dinghy which will almost certainly be equipped with a *Standing Lugsail*.

We can see from the illustration opposite that the Standing Lugsail has four sides. The long forward edge, known as the *head*, is attached to a spar called the *yard*. The bottom edge, or *foot*, is also attached to a spar which is referred to as the *boom*, and this is loosely connected to the mast by the *goose-neck* which allows the boom to swivel freely from side to side. The short edge of the sail between the head and the foot is called the *luff* while the long after length extending from the pointed top, or *peak*, of the sail to the foot is known as the *leech*.

On two-sail dinghies a small triangular sail, the *foresail* or *jib*, is carried forward of the mast. The mainsail may then be another four-sided design called a *Gaff*, a variation of it, the *Gunter*, or a triangular *Bermudan*. The Bermudan will not normally be found on the very small dinghies but it is interesting to be able to recognise the various types.

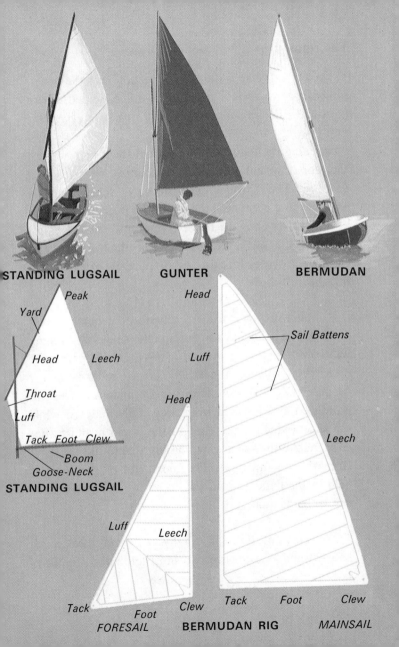

STANDING LUGSAIL

GUNTER

BERMUDAN

Peak

Yard

Head

Sail Battens

Head

Luff

Leech

Throat

Luff

Head

Leech

Tack Foot Clew

Boom

Goose-Neck

STANDING LUGSAIL

Luff

Leech

Tack

Foot

Clew

FORESAIL

Tack

Foot

Clew

BERMUDAN RIG

MAINSAIL

The rigging

The term *rigging* is used in connection with the ropes, or *cordage*, with which a sailing boat is equipped. There are two kinds; *standing rigging* and *running rigging*.

Standing rigging is used to support the mast and, in a small boat, would normally consist of two *shrouds* and a *forestay*. The shrouds give sideways support, being attached to a point near the top of the mast and secured, at their lower ends, to bottle screws and shroud plates on either side of the hull to tension the rigging. The forestay provides fore and aft support and extends from masthead to bow.

Running rigging is used to actually control the movement of the sails and for our simple, single-sail dinghy will consist of a *halyard* and a *sheet*. In this particular case, they will be the *main halyard* and *mainsheet* because they will control the single mainsail. The sail is hoisted and lowered by means of the halyard while the sheet, which is attached to the boom near its after end, enables the sail angle to be adjusted to suit the wind strength and direction. The loose end of the sheet is held in the hand so that the necessary sail adjustments can be made quickly.

The two-sail type of dinghy will also have a jib halyard and two jibsheets to hoist and adjust the fore-sail.

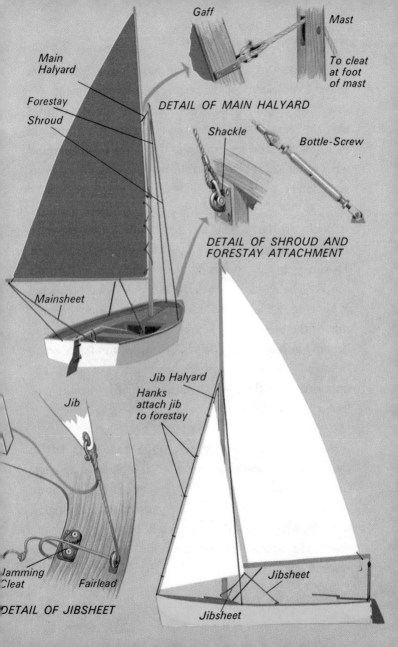

Main Halyard

Forestay

Shroud

Gaff

Mast

To cleat at foot of mast

DETAIL OF MAIN HALYARD

Shackle

Bottle-Screw

DETAIL OF SHROUD AND FORESTAY ATTACHMENT

Mainsheet

Jib

Jamming Cleat

Fairlead

DETAIL OF JIBSHEET

Jib Halyard

Hanks attach jib to forestay

Jibsheet

Jibsheet

Describing wind direction

The previous chapters will have given you some general knowledge of the dinghy and its equipment. We can now begin to consider the craft in its natural elements of wind and water, and here again we must get to know the correct language if we are to understand what other sailors say and follow the sailing instructions given later.

We know that a boat has a port side and a starboard side. In sailing, it also has a *weather* side and a *lee* side. This may appear confusing at first but it is really quite simple. The weather side is the side onto which the wind is blowing, while the lee side is the opposite or sheltered side of the boat. There is another distinction: if you are heading into the wind, that is—the direction from which the wind is blowing, you are heading to *windward*. The opposite direction is *leeward* (actually pronounced loo'ard).

Wind blowing directly across the boat from left to right is said to be on the *port beam*, if it blows at an angle from in front it is on the *port bow*, and if it blows at an angle from behind it is on the *port quarter*. Similarly, wind blowing from right to left will be on the *starboard beam*, the *starboard bow* and the *starboard quarter* respectively.

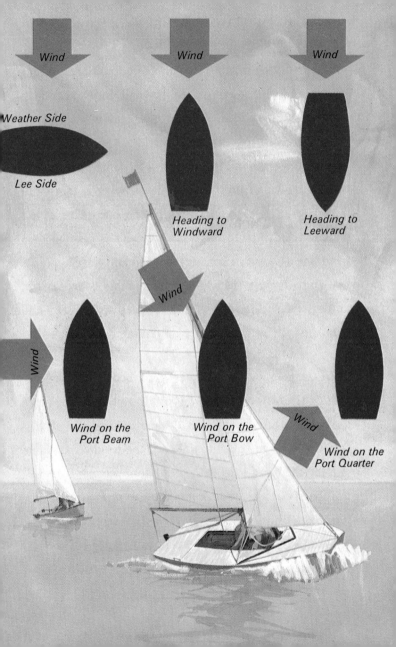

Wind

Wind

Wind

Weather Side

Lee Side

Heading to
Windward

Heading to
Leeward

Wind

Wind

Wind

Wind on the
Port Beam

Wind on the
Port Bow

Wind on the
Port Quarter

Points of sailing—close-hauling

The first thing we must remember about sailing is that a boat cannot sail directly into the wind. In the head-to-wind position the sail simply flaps and is unable to propel the craft forward. You might ask what happens when you wish to sail from point X to point Y when the wind is blowing from Y to X? The answer is that you must steer a zig-zag course first to one side of the wind direction and then to the other, keeping as *close* to the wind line as you can with the sail full and not flapping. If it starts to flap, the angle of travel must be increased until it fills again. Eventually, after a series of such manoeuvres you will reach your aiming point at Y.

Zig-zagging in the manner described is known as *beating to windward* or *tacking*. While sailing in this way the boat is said to be *close-hauled*, and this is one of the three main points of sailing. When the wind strikes the sail on the port side with the boom angled over to starboard we can say we are on the *port tack*; wind from starboard and boom to port is the *starboard tack*. Normally, an angle of at least forty-five degrees to the wind direction is as close as an average boat will sail.

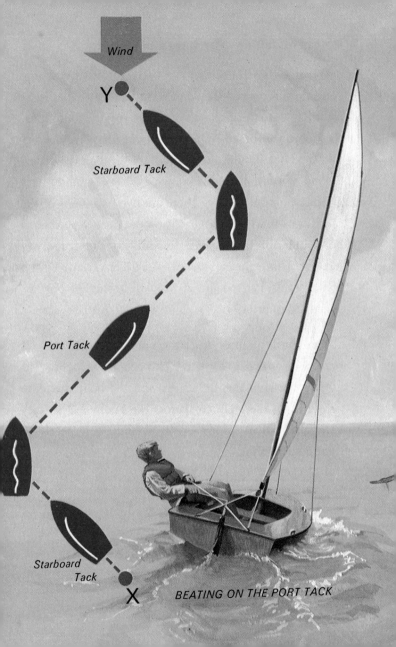

Wind

Y

Starboard Tack

Port Tack

Starboard
Tack

X

BEATING ON THE PORT TACK

Points of sailing—reaching and running

Generally speaking, the most straightforward sailing conditions are when the wind is on the beam, that is, at right-angles to the direction of travel. In such conditions, the boom will be angled out at about forty-five degrees and the boat should move smoothly through the water. Sailing in a beam wind is known as *reaching*, and this is another point of sailing. There are two variations of the reach: one is when the wind is on the port or starboard bow, but not far enough forward to call for close-hauling. This is the *close reach*. The other variation is the *broad reach*, i.e., when the wind is from the port or starboard quarter.

The third point of sailing we are concerned with is *running* or *sailing off the wind*. This occurs when the wind is blowing from the stern area and the boat is sailing before it. In these circumstances the boom will usually be angled out as far as it will go until it is nearly at right-angles to the boat.

Running is not quite the "plain sailing" that it appears, as we shall see. The wind direction can be critical and unless the correct line is steered relative to the wind, the boom may unexpectedly swing right across to the other side of the boat, possibly capsizing it.

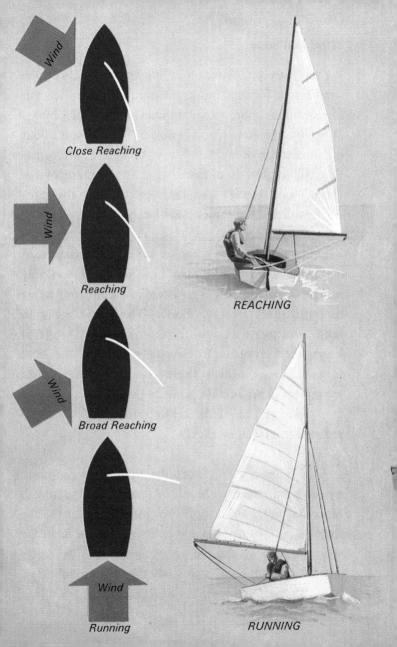

Close Reaching

Reaching

Broad Reaching

Running

Wind

Wind

Wind

Wind

REACHING

RUNNING

Wind and sails

Everybody knows that a sailing boat depends on the wind for its forward movement through the water, but there is much more to sailing than simply being blown along. It is therefore worth finding out a little more about the interaction of wind and sails, because this information will enable us to understand the purpose of the various sail settings and help us to make the most efficient use of the forces available.

In fact, a sail acts in a similar way to a single-surfaced aeroplane wing, except that it is mounted vertically instead of horizontally. The forces of *lift* and *drag* apply to both. (See 'How it Works—The Aeroplane'.) In both cases lift is a useful force provided by the air; it keeps the aeroplane flying and it propels the boat forward. Drag, which causes resistance to forward movement in an aircraft, tends to push a boat sideways in the water. Use of the centreboard greatly helps to reduce this unwanted effect.

A sail must not only catch the air currents produced by the wind, it must also allow them to escape and so make way for a fresh supply of fast-moving air to take their place, thus maintaining an uninterrupted flow. On the next page we can see just what happens to the air when it meets the sail, and study the forces involved.

18

The curve of the sail deflects the flow of air, setting up a local increase of pressure to windward and a decrease of pressure to leeward. This difference in pressure results in the 'LIFT' which propels the boat forward.

How a sail works

Let us first take the most simple point of sailing—reaching in a beam wind. The flow of air from A (diagram 1 opposite) strikes the angled sail at B. In doing so it pushes the sail outward, loses some of its speed and is deflected toward the stern in direction C. The forces AB and BC behind the sail set up two other forces in front of it, namely BD and BE. Force BD is the outward pressure on the sail which causes drag and the tendency of the boat to slip sideways. As mentioned before, this must be restricted by the centreboard. However, force BD is not entirely counteracted by the centreboard and the boat will travel in the direction of the arrow F, which is inclined at a small angle to leeward of the boat's centreline. This small angle is known as the *leeway*, (diagram 2). Force BE is not restricted and provides the lift which propels the boat forward.

In beating to windward, the wind strikes the closely-trimmed sail at a much narrower angle and there is less sail area available to catch it. The same forces apply as before but if we look at diagram 3 we see that the drag (line BD) is much greater than the lift (line BE). This means that in the close-hauled condition there is far less useful force obtainable for forward movement and so the leeway angle is increased and the speed of the dinghy will be considerably reduced as compared with reaching.

When running with the wind astern, (diagram 4) there is little sideways drag and nearly all the wind's force is available to drive the boat forward.

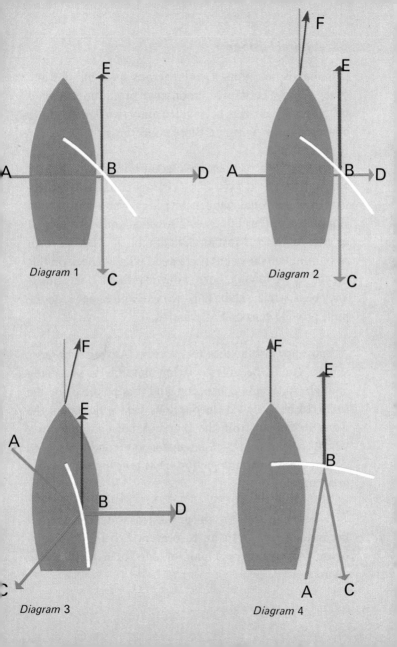

Diagram 1

Diagram 2

Diagram 3

Diagram 4

Safety precautions

Sailing is not, in itself, a dangerous sport but like any other activity certain commonsense precautions should be taken. These can be divided into two kinds; those concerning the boat and those concerning the crew.

Firstly, the boat must have good buoyancy so that it will remain afloat even if it becomes completely water-logged. This could happen in rough water with waves slopping over the gunwales, following damage to the hull or after a capsize. Most modern dinghies have some form of built-in buoyancy but it is a good plan to check on this aspect before buying, borrowing or hiring a boat. Buoyancy bags, which can be filled with air and attached to the hull, provide a second alternative.

Buoyancy also applies to the crew. Anyone who goes sailing should be able to swim, but this is not really enough. Accidents can occur, and it is possible for the sailor to be knocked unconscious before he enters the water or far out from the shore. A personal life-jacket which will keep him afloat under any conditions is an essential piece of sailing equipment and should be worn at all times.

A baler to get rid of unwanted water is another necessary item. Tie it on to prevent it being lost over-board. Always carry a pair of oars or a paddle, and an anchor.

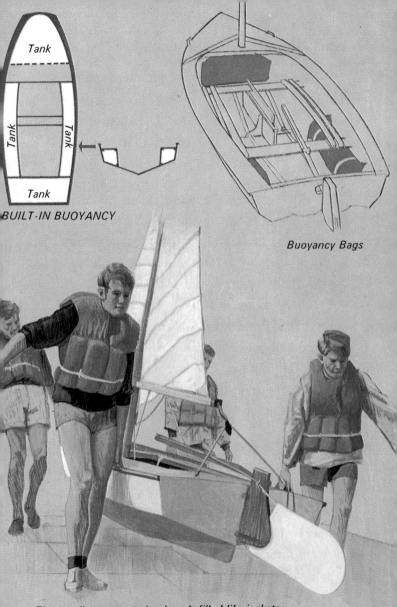

BUILT-IN BUOYANCY

Buoyancy Bags

These sailors are wearing kapok-filled life-jackets which will stay afloat almost indefinitely.

Where to start

We are now nearly ready to get afloat and enjoy our first sailing experience. But where do we start? On the sea? In a harbour? On a river? On a lake or reservoir? The choice is wide and varied so let us take each suggestion in turn.

The sea is perhaps the most obvious choice and on a calm day with a light breeze blowing is quite suitable. On the other hand, choppy conditions which may add to the pleasure of a good sailor can create additional complications for the novice. Harbours are usually calm but inclined to be used by a great many other craft plying to and fro and the traffic can be distracting. River sailing usually involves manoeuvring across the stream with the frequent putting about and sail adjustment that this requires—enjoyable for people with some sailing experience but confusing for the beginner.

Lakes and reservoirs seem to provide the ideal sailing conditions for the beginner. The water is normally smooth and there is plenty of space for trying out the various points of sailing and making the inevitable mistakes. It is appreciated, however, that we have to start our sailing at a place we can conveniently get to, even though it may not be exactly what we might choose.

Getting afloat

We will assume that your dinghy is new and that you have followed the instructions to raise, or *step*, the mast and secure the shrouds, and that the sail with its yard, if it has one, and boom is on board ready for hoisting. The halyard with which you will hoist the sail is secured to a *cleat*, like a double-sided hook, at the foot of the mast. The halyard should not be knotted round the cleat but tied with one or two figure of eight turns finishing with a loop tucked under the last turn. This allows it to be *let go* at a moment's notice.

A block is shackled to a metal rail (the *sheet horse*) above the transom and the sheet is attached to it. The sheet passes through a block attached to the boom and thence back through the block on the sheet horse to the hand. A stop-knot (figure of eight) should be tied at the end of the sheet to prevent it from slipping through the pulley block (see page 50).

The dinghy can now be pushed into the water and you can get aboard. Before hoisting the sail, make sure that the dinghy is heading as nearly as possible into the wind so that it will not start sailing away until you are ready. With the sail hoisted but not catching the wind, put the rudder in position on its pintles, or if you have a hinged rudder which is already on its pintles drop this into position, and fit the tiller.

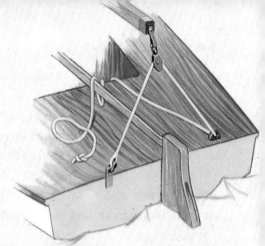

SECURING A HALYARD
TO A CLEAT

ARRANGEMENT OF THE MAINSHEET

Sheet Horse

MAINSHEET ARRANGEMENT WITH A SHEET HORSE

Controlling the boat

There are three means by which a single-sail dinghy is controlled, namely, the tiller, the mainsheet and the centreboard. The tiller and sheet will be in constant use, the one to maintain or change direction, the other to adjust and *trim* the sail. Therefore these two are held one in each hand. The centreboard requires less frequent attention, and one hand may be freed to adjust it by momentarily transferring the sheet to the hand holding the tiller.

One important thing to remember when steering is that the dinghy will turn in the direction in which the rudder blade is pointing. That means you must move the tiller in the opposite direction. So, if you want to turn to port, you angle the rudder to port by moving the tiller to starboard.

Take up a position toward the stern of the dinghy with your back to the wind, one hand holding the tiller, the other holding the sheet. When the wind strikes the sail it will cause the boat to lean to leeward and the weight of your body on the windward side will help to counterbalance this effect. Boats sail best when leaning slightly but if allowed to go over too far, water will enter over the gunwale. Keep your dinghy reasonably upright by leaning your body further over to windward as necessary.

Sailing on a reach

When you are comfortably settled, pull the sheet halfway in and turn the boat until the wind is on the beam and filling the sail (see page 46, 'Rowing'). As she starts moving ahead you will notice a tendency for the bows to turn into the wind. This is quite normal and it can be corrected by *putting your helm up*, that is, moving your tiller to windward. You are now sailing on a reach, or reaching. If the wind is fairly fresh, put the centreboard about three-quarters down and concentrate on steering a straight course, using a light touch on the tiller. Never grip it tightly.

As you move away from the shore you may find that the wind strengthens and that your body weight is not sufficient to counteract the boat's tendency to lean over. In such an event, ease the sail out a little by letting a few inches of sheet slip slowly through your hand. The increased sail angle will offer less resistance to the wind and the boat will right itself.

If you meet an occasional extra-strong gust of wind, ease the sail as described but also turn the bows a little to windward by *putting your helm down* (moving the tiller to leeward) an inch or two. This manoeuvre is known as *luffing*. Return to your original line when the gust subsides.

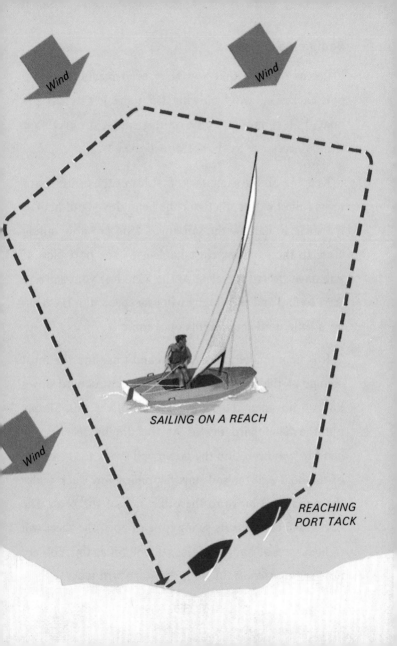

Wind

Wind

Wind

SAILING ON A REACH

*REACHING
PORT TACK*

Sailing close-hauled

Let us imagine that you have been reaching on the port tack, i.e., wind blowing from the left across the boat. You cannot continue on this course for ever so it will be necessary to change direction.

Keeping on the same tack, first lower the centreboard to its fullest extent, then put the helm down and haul in the sheet to narrow the sail angle. You are now sailing close to the wind, or close-hauled, on the port tack. If you have steered too close to the wind line your sail will start to flap and the dinghy will lose speed. Put the helm up a little until the sail fills once more.

It is time to alter course again and this time you must change to the other tack. Leave the centreboard down and do not alter the angle, or trim, of the sail. Simply put the helm hard down. As the dinghy reaches the head-to-wind position the boom will swing to the centre of the boat and the sail start flapping. Now duck under the boom and move to the other side of the boat. The boom will continue its swing over to port, the sheet will tighten in your hand and the sail will fill again. You are now sailing close-hauled on the starboard tack.

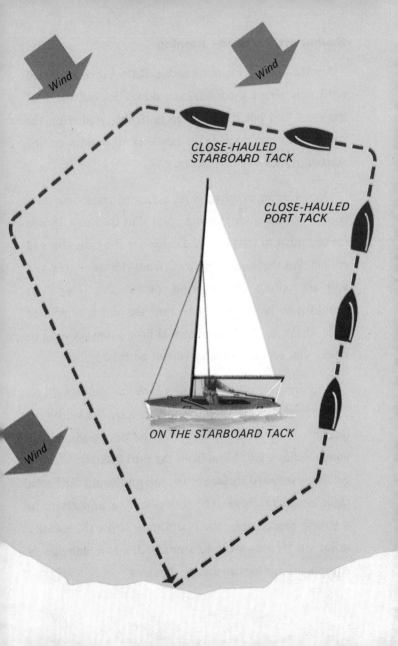

Sailing off the wind—running

Another change of course is due. Raise the centreboard until it is about three-quarters down, let out more of the sheet and put the helm up until the wind is on the beam. You are once again reaching, this time on the starboard tack.

One more manoeuvre is necessary to bring you on a course back to your starting point. Put the helm up and make a turn to port. As you complete the turn you will realise that the wind is blowing from the stern area and you are sailing off the wind, or running. The sheet should now be let right out until the sail is almost at right-angles to the boat. There is little sideways drag to worry you so the centreboard can be raised.

You are now all set for the run home, but watch it! Try to steer so as to keep the wind toward the starboard quarter. If the boom is out over the port side and the wind is allowed to blow from the port quarter, it could catch the forward surface of the sail and swing the boom right across the boat. The results can be unpleasant in a strong breeze since the boom may strike the unwary sailor on its way over to starboard, cause damage to equipment and/or capsize the boat.

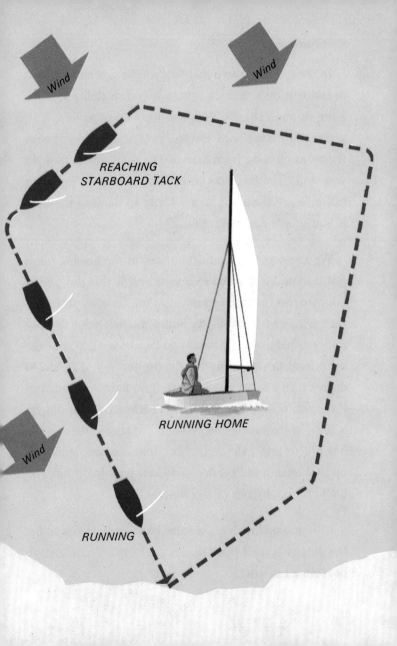

Bringing-up

In the previous three chapters you have been making a round trip on a lake or calm sea and in doing so have gone through the most common points of sailing. You are now running back toward your starting point with the wind blowing from astern. The question is, how do you stop? The boat has no brakes, there is no motor to put into reverse and you are likely to damage the boat if you simply run it aground.

We know that a boat cannot sail in the head-to-wind position and will come to a standstill if this position is adopted. So to stop, or *bring-up*, your dinghy you must turn her head-to-wind. As you approach your landing and you judge your position to be about right, put the helm hard down, swing the dinghy through a tight 180 degree turn and let go the sheet. You have stopped, and if the manoeuvre has been gauged correctly your dinghy will be in shallow water, close to the shore. Release the halyard to lower the sail, check that the centreboard is up and unship the rudder. You can now jump out and haul the dinghy out of the water.

Bringing-up involves the same basic operation whether the dinghy is used from the shore, from a landing stage or from a mooring.

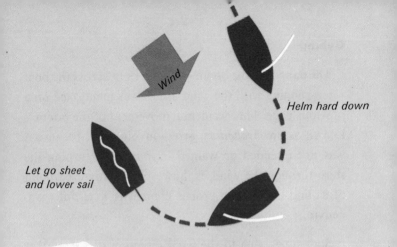

Wind

Helm hard down

Let go sheet and lower sail

BRINGING-UP AFTER THE ROUND TRIP

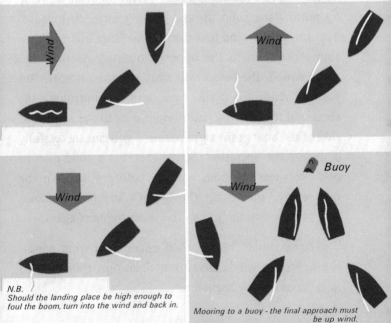

Wind

Wind

Wind

Wind

Buoy

N.B.
Should the landing place be high enough to foul the boom, turn into the wind and back in.

Mooring to a buoy - the final approach must be up wind.

In all cases ease the sheets on approach to reduce speed

BRINGING-UP WITH THE WIND IN OTHER DIRECTIONS

Gybing

The danger of the boom swinging right across the boat when running with the wind astern was mentioned on a previous page. This accidental movement of the boom is known as an *involuntary gybe*—involuntary, because it was not intended or wanted. *Gybing*, i.e., turning the stern through the wind, is, however, a recognized point of sailing and under proper control is a useful manoeuvre.

Sometimes, due to the wind direction or some other reason, it is not possible to alter course in the usual way by tacking to windward, so the alteration must be made by putting the helm up and turning away to leeward. This brings the wind first over the weather quarter, then round the stern to the opposite quarter. As the wind shifts round, the boom will start swinging across. But you are ready for it this time, and by controlling the sheet and transferring your weight over to the windward side of the boat at the right moment you can successfully complete the operation. Sometimes it is a good plan to pull the sheet in about halfway before you begin the manoeuvre, shortening the boom's swinging distance and so reducing the jolt as the sheet tightens again.

Gybing should be practised under light wind conditions. Strong winds make the operation difficult and hazardous for the beginner.

Wind

Two sails

So far we have dealt almost entirely with the single-sail dinghy because the principles of sailing are easier to understand in a craft of this type. However, there are a greater number of two-sail dinghies in general use so we should take a brief look at their operation.

Although a two-sail dinghy can be sailed single-handed, especially by an experienced sailor, it normally takes two people to sail it: a helmsman and crew. The helmsman is in command of the boat and controls the tiller and mainsheet. The crew usually looks after the port and starboard jibsheets which control the foresail, and adjusts the centreboard as required.

The jib is always trimmed by means of the leeward sheet; the windward sheet being kept fairly slack during normal sailing. An exception to this rule is when the boat's speed has to be reduced to avoid another craft crossing its bows or for bringing-up. The windward sheet must then be hauled in, 'backing' the jib.

Always set the jib so that its foot is angled on the same line as the foot of the mainsail to ensure that the air flows smoothly between the two sails. It is not usually necessary to alter the trim of the jib as long as you are sailing a straight course.

Windward
Sheet

Leeward
Sheet

Wind

Getting-Away

Wind

Jib backed
Main lowered

Bringing-Up

BACKING THE JIB

Trimming the jib

The first thing to know is that the mainsail of a two-sail dinghy is adjusted in exactly the same way as the mainsail of a single-sail craft for the various points of sailing. We can therefore leave this out of our reckoning and study the principles applied to trimming the jib, although experience alone will tell you exactly how much sheet is needed to propel the boat along at its best speed.

When sailing close-hauled, the jibsheet should be pulled fairly well in. If the mainsail luff begins to flap or lift, the jibsheet is too tight and should be let out a little until the mainsail luff becomes steady again. When reaching, the jib can be angled out further, so the sheet should be slowly let out as necessary.

Running with the wind astern requires a different technique. On this point of sailing the widely-angled mainsail completely 'blankets' off the jib and prevents the wind from getting to it. Under these circumstances it must be trimmed to work on the side opposite to the mainsail. This is helped if the jib is *boomed out* by fitting one end of a thin pole into the *clew* (the after point at the foot of the sail). The other end of the pole can be held in the hand or lashed to the mast. The jib is thus pushed out sideways.

Wrong
Jibsheet too tight, restricting flow of air between sails.

Right
Free flow of air between sails.

TRIMMING THE JIB

JIB BLANKETED BY MAINSAIL

RUNNING 'GOOSEWINGED'

Capsize

Accidents happen in the best regulated circles and, in sailing, the worst that can normally occur is a capsize. This is not a pleasant experience, especially if the water is cold, but it need not be particularly dangerous if the correct procedures are followed.

The most common cause of capsizing is a very strong gust of wind which overcomes the boat's built-in stability and the efforts of the crew to keep her upright. She will lean too far over to leeward and not be able to recover. Generally speaking she will lie on her side prevented by her mast and sails from turning upside down. Under these conditions the dinghy can sometimes be righted if you put all your weight on the centreboard, and it is a good plan to lower the mainsail so that there is less resistance to your efforts. Once righted, the dinghy will float, though full of water, due to its buoyancy. Untie the baler, bale out the water and away you go.

If you are not able to right the dinghy, stay with her, hanging on to the most convenient part. The shore always appears nearer than it actually is and reaching it may be beyond your powers of swimming. Also, it is easier for your rescuers to spot the comparatively large dinghy than a small head above the water.

ABOUT TO CAPSIZE
This could have been avoided
by easing the mainsheet
before she heeled over so far.

With one crew member on the
centreboard and the other in the
water to steady her, she will
soon be righted.

Rowing

Rowing is, of course, a pastime in itself—as is canoeing—but it can also play an important part in sailing as a means of auxiliary power. Always carry a pair of oars or a paddle with you in the dinghy.

When your dinghy is launched head-to-wind and the sail is hoisted, a brief pull with an oar may be necessary to bring the bows round and so enable you to start sailing. The rudder cannot steer the boat until she is under way. You may also be caught in the head-to-wind position during a change of tack if the manoeuvre has not been correctly carried out. A quick stroke or two will get you going again. You may misjudge bringing up the dinghy after a sail and have to row the remaining distance into shallow water. Oars are also useful if the wind drops and leaves you becalmed or, conversely, if it suddenly blows too strongly and you have to lower the mainsail to avoid the likelihood of capsizing.

Some dinghies are provided with *rowlocks* which support the oars on the gunwales and provide a fulcrum to pull against; if your dinghy has no rowlocks, you should use a paddle. When rowing, the oar blades should be in the vertical position and completely covered by the water—though not too deeply If they are allowed to come out of the water halfway through a stroke you will *catch a crab*.

Blades vertical 2" above water.   2   Lower blades into water.   3   Pull back with trunk, arms straight.

4   Complete stroke by bending elbows. Blades should now be at 45° and just clear of water.

5   Drop hands to raise oars. Drop wrists to turn blade to horizontal.

6   Push arms forward, then trunk, to reach position 1.

THE ROWING STROKE CYCLE

With a helmsman you can paddle from the bow. If alone, you can paddle a straight course only stern first.

Under power

For those who enjoy messing about in boats but prefer a powered craft, there is a very wide choice of outboard motors, many of them suitable for the general size of dinghy which you have been reading about. Make sure you obtain the right type of motor for the boat you have in mind. Hulls are designed to give a certain maximum speed and no matter how powerful the motor, the boat will travel no faster than it is designed to do. Unnecessary power is wasteful.

Outboards work on the same basic principles as engines fitted to motor cycles. They may have one or more pistons and operate on the two-stroke or four-stroke system. (See 'How it Works—The Motor Cycle'.) The drive is taken by a shaft from the motor itself down to a gearbox which turns it through a right-angle so that it can rotate the propeller. Some motors also have forward, neutral and reverse gears. There is no rudder as such, the whole motor being swivelled on its bracket to steer the boat. The short tiller usually incorporates a twist-grip arrangement for opening and closing the throttle.

When navigating in restricted waters, remember that priority must be given to sailing craft, though in a channel a vessel with deep draught *must* stay in the channel. In all other cases keep to the right and pass oncoming boats port side to port side.

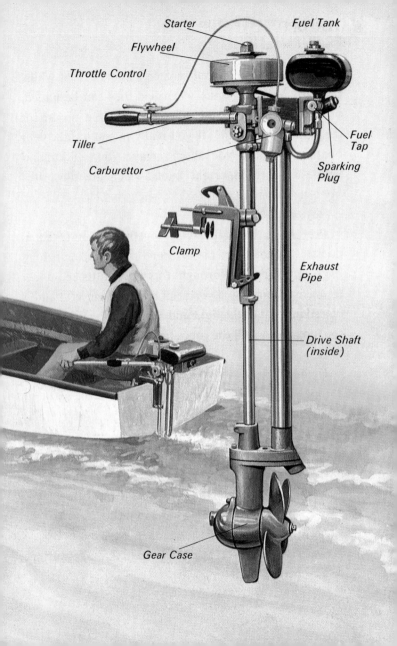

Starter

Fuel Tank

Flywheel

Throttle Control

Tiller

Carburettor

Fuel Tap

Sparking Plug

Clamp

Exhaust Pipe

Drive Shaft (inside)

Gear Case

Some useful knots

The great advantage of seamen's knots is that whilst they are perfectly secure when tied they can be untied, or *cast off*, quickly and easily. A seaman has no use for the common 'grannie'. If you really intend to take your boating seriously you should make yourself familiar with the most important knots which are illustrated opposite.

Reef Knot. Used for tying together ropes of equal thickness. The end of the left-hand rope is taken behind the right-hand piece, brought forward and tucked under to make the first twist. The end now in your left hand is placed in front of the right and brought forward through the loop. Now pull the ropes tight.

Figure of Eight. A stop knot tied to prevent the end of a rope from slipping through a pulley block or other small space. The *Bowline* is used to make a loop. It has many purposes, one of the most important being a safety line fitted round a crew member's waist. A *Sheetbend* is used to tie a rope end to a loop and to join two ropes of unequal thickness. With the *Clove Hitch* a rope can be tied (*made fast*) to a mooring post, and the *Rolling Hitch* would be used on a horizontal bar. A *Round Turn and Two Half Hitches* will make fast a rope to any bar or ring.

50

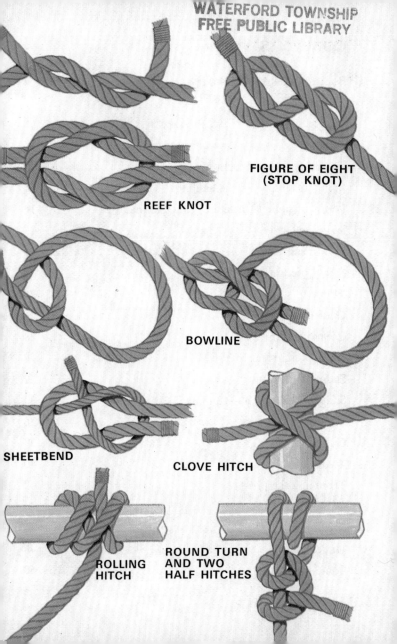

FIGURE OF EIGHT
(STOP KNOT)

REEF KNOT

BOWLINE

SHEETBEND

CLOVE HITCH

ROLLING
HITCH

ROUND TURN
AND TWO
HALF HITCHES

CONTENTS